My Grandma is Like the
Sea

Written by Natalie Frańćeska
Illustrated by Sanja Kolenko

nala's den

To my loving late grandmothers, whose love and connection to the wisdom of the sea have forever left a mark on me.

For my son, Ivo.
N. F.

My Grandma is Like the Sea flowed effortlessly. It was written straight from the heart.

It is inspired by childhood memories of long summers spent at my grandparents' homes in Korčula and Mali Ston and with family in Dubrovnik on the southern Dalmatian coast in Croatia. The illustrations are reflective of the cultural influence of the region.

The illustration of the female folk costume from the city of Ston was created in accordance with the watercolour template *DUM EM 1617, Donna di Stagno* (Woman from Ston) from the museum collection *Costumi dei dintorni di Ragusa* (Costumes from Dubrovnik surroundings) by Salvatore Cofsich, 1880. This collection was graciously provided by Dubrovnik Museums - Ethnographic Museum.

May children from all over the world feel inspired by this timeless, magical book.

I would love to see pictures of all the places around the world where you are reading *My Grandma is Like the Sea*.
Tag me on social media!

 @natiefranceska

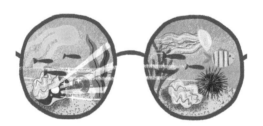

First Published in 2021 by Nala's Den
© Natalie Frančeska 2021

ISBN: 978-0-6450254-0-8 (Paperback)
ISBN: 978-0-6450254-2-2 (Hardcover)
ISBN: 978-0-6450254-7-7 (eBook)
© Text copyright 2021 by Natalie Frančeska
© Illustrations copyright 2021 by Sanja Kolenko
First Edition

 A catalogue record for this work is available from the National Library of Australia

www.nalasden.com

My grandma is like the sea,
flowing with love and purity.
She brings so much joy to me.

With light in her eyes
and with wrinkles of age,
she glistens like a million specks of sparkly sand,
glowing on centre stage.

Her hands tell a story,
like a well-travelled wave
carrying memories of a life so grand.

She's always been so brave.

The scent of lavender and pine
follows her around.
The island of her birth
reminds me of a playground.

On my grandmother's island, explorers meet,
then sail far, far away.
Like the great Marco Polo!
Well, that's what they say.

Marco!

Polo!

Grandma spins me around in circles.
Sometimes, it makes me dizzy.

But she catches me before I fall.
Singing and dancing keep us busy.

She's as fun as fun can be.
She's as wise as an owl.
When Grandma tells me stories,
she wraps me up in a cosy towel.

As we sit at the beach,
by the big blue sea,
Grandma squints her shiny eyes
and then exclaims to me ...

'Be free, be bold, and make a SPLASH!
Do not be afraid!'

'If I'm not with you always, it's because I'm sitting in the shade.'

'But I'm still watching you grow, and my nurturing waters remain.'

'Just be sure whatever you do that it isn't in vain.'

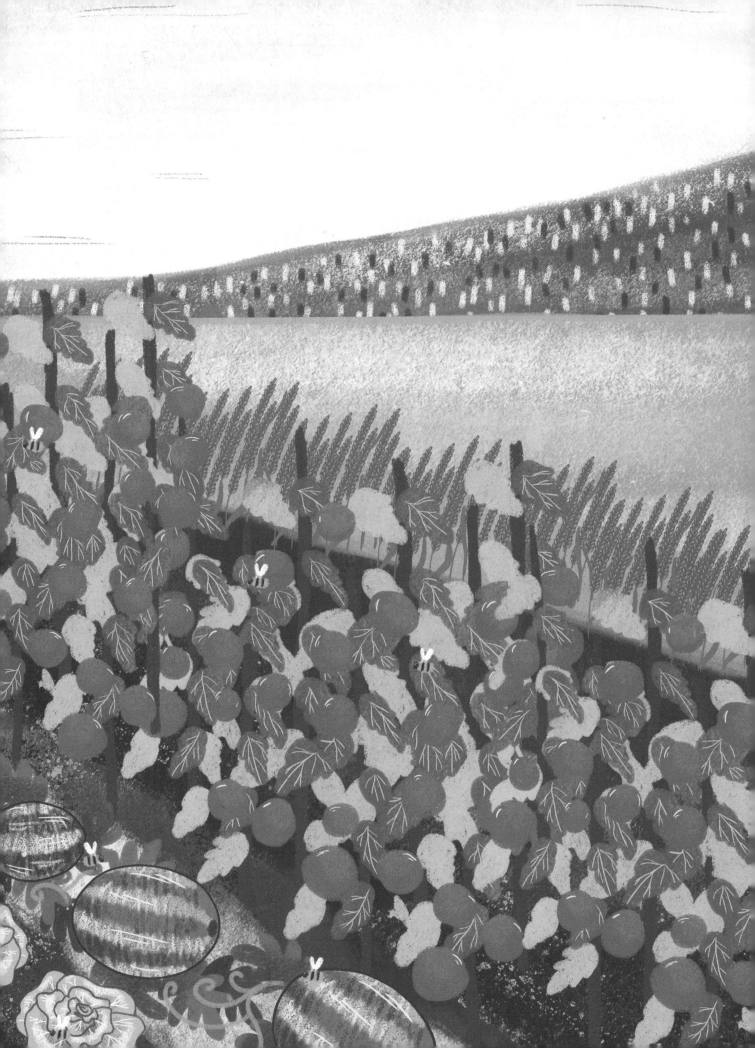

Like the whoosh and roar of a wave,
Grandma's cuddle surrounds me.
Then she goes on to say ...

'The magic is in the moment, my dear.
It's always right in front of you.'

My grandma goes on to teach me
about the tides
and all the beautiful fish in the sea.

'Don't fight against the current,' Grandma explains to me.

'Sail towards what your heart desires.
Have fun, and don't forget to giggle!
But if you ever tire,
remember ... '

'I carry you in my heart, where you can rest.
Like a harbour, it's the safest place to be.'

'But sometimes, we must voyage out
in search of the glistening treasure chest
in the depths of the big blue sea.'

'And while you're on your travels,
I'll be at the shore, waiting for you
with open arms and a love so deep.'

CPSIA information can be obtained
at www.ICGtesting.com
Printed in the USA
LVHW070357220921
698427LV00002B/42